I0606889

David Laing

Biographical Notices of Thomas Young

David Laing

Biographical Notices of Thomas Young

ISBN/EAN: 9783742813831

Manufactured in Europe, USA, Canada, Australia, Japa

Cover: Foto ©Andreas Hilbeck / pixelio.de

Manufactured and distributed by brebook publishing software
(www.brebook.com)

David Laing

Biographical Notices of Thomas Young

BIOGRAPHICAL NOTICES

OF

THOMAS YOUNG, S.T.D.

VICAR OF STOWMARKET, SUFFOLK.

BY

THE EDITOR OF PRINCIPAL BAILLIE'S
"LETTERS AND JOURNALS."

EDINBURGH: MDCCCLXX.

The following Notices were designed for the Appendix to Vol. III.
of the " Letters and Journals of Principal Baillie," published in
1842. Owing to the increased size of that volume, the proposed
article was withheld. Intending, however, to use this brief memoir
in some other form, it was enlarged, chiefly from the information
furnished by a valuable local work not much known, the Rev. Mr
Hollingsworth's *" History of Stowmarket, the Ancient County*
Town of Suffolk," printed at Ipswich, 1844, 4to.

The Annual Meeting of the Archæological Institute, to be held
this month at Bury St Edmunds, brought these notices to my
recollection ; and as the learned divine, Dr Young, may be reckoned
one of the Suffolk Worthies, it occurred to me that it might gratify
some of the members by having a few copies printed for private
circulation.

David Laing.

Edinburgh, *July* 1869.

BIOGRAPHICAL NOTICES

THOMAS YOUNG, S.T.D.

Dr Thomas Young, a celebrated Puritan divine, who is occasionally mentioned by Baillie,[1] was a native of Scotland. According to his monumental inscription in the church of Stowmarket,[2] of which he became Vicar, the date of his birth was the year 1587. In his *Dies Dominica*, which appeared in 1639, he styles himself *Theophilus Philo-Kuriaces Loncardiensis*, and this enables us to ascertain his birth-place, while it leaves no doubt that his father was William Young, minister of the united parishes of Loncardy and Redgorton, in Perthshire.

On examining the Registers of "Assignations and Modifications of Stipends," it appears that Andrew Colt was minister of Ragorton and Loncardie in the years 1574 to 1580; and that William Young was reader at Loncardy from 1576. On a division of these parishes, Young became minister of Loncardy, as Colt's successor, in 1581; and on the 8th February 1582-83, he obtained a presentation to "the personage and vicarage of the paroche kirke of Loncardy," vacant by demission of Master Walter Balfour, last permanent vicar and possessor. From the Register of Assignations, in 1593, it appears that on Colt's death or resignation Loncardy and Ragorton were again united, and that William Young, as minister, had for his stipend : "The haill personage and vicarage of Loncardy, L.26, 13s. 4d.; The haill vicarage of Ragorton, L.5, 6s. 8d; and out of the Thirds of the Abbey of Scone,

---

[1] Letters and Journals, vol. i. p. 366 ; vol. ii. pp. 110, 118, 140, 148, 336; vol. iii. pp. 302, 306. Edinburgh, 1841, 1842. 3 vols. 4to., or roy. 8vo.

[2] The Suffolk Garland. &c., p. 284. Ipswich, 1818. 8vo.

L.29, 13s. 4d., and x bolles beir, viij bolles meill, with manse
and gleib, and kirkland of Loncardy."[1] Few country parishes were
so well provided. William Young was one of forty-two ministers
who signed the protestation offered to Parliament against the
pre-eminence of bishops and introduction of Episcopacy into Scotland, 1st July 1606.[2] But he latterly conformed to the innovations then forced upon the Church. He continued minister of the
parish till his death, before the 30th of November 1625, and
was succeeded in February 1626 by his son-in-law, Mr John
Cruickshank.

Thomas Young, after having received a classical education at
the Grammar School of Perth, was sent to the University of
St Andrews. The year 1602 would be the time of his matricula-
tion, as the course of philosophical study extended over four
years ; and in the College Registers, his name, THOMAS JUNIUS,
occurs as one of eighteen students styled *minus potentes Magis-
trandi* (or, the less opulent), who obtained the degree of Master
of Arts in July 1606.

It has not been ascertained when or where Young completed his
theological studies, and was licensed as a minister. His father
had probably one or more sons in the ministry, and may have
sent Thomas to one of the Protestant Universities of Northern
Germany. But for several years we have no information respecting his mode of life or employment. We can only conjecture
that he had either been engaged in private tuition, or as an
assistant to some of the Puritan ministers in England, at the time

[1] The village of Loncardy or Luncarty, in the neighbourhood of Perth, is
celebrated in history as the site of a battle with the Danes, at the end of the
tenth century. For many years after the Reformation, the difficulty of ob-
taining a sufficient number of qualified persons for the ministry, led to the
uniting of two or more parishes into one (a measure, perhaps, justifiable at
the time, but found to be very prejudicial). In April 1612, the Synod of
Fife, "considering how gryt ane hinderance to the Gospel is brought be
the pluralitie of Kirkis servit be ane persone," appointed a committee to
inquire into the state of the parishes in their bounds. Among other
instances they found " Loncardie, Pitcairnes, and Redgortoune, in the
persone of William Young."

[2] Printed in Row's History of the Kirk of Scotland (Wodrow Society
edition, pp. 424–436). Edinb. 1842. 8vo.

it was his good fortune to be entrusted with training the youthful mind of England's great poet, the author of "Paradise Lost." This was in the year 1618, when Milton had reached the tenth year of his age; and their connexion subsisted for nearly five years, while the influence which he exercised on the mind of such a youth was not limited to mere proficiency in classical learning. In his *Liber Epistolarum*, Milton has preserved two letters which he addressed to his tutor, in terms of affectionate kindness alike honourable to both. On Young's change of residence by a foreign appointment, the youthful poet was next placed at St Paul's School, of which Alexander Gill was master. In less than twelve months Milton was sent to Cambridge, having been admitted in Christ's College on the 12th February 1624.[1]

At a later period of life, Milton, in order to vindicate himself from some malicious slanders, thus adverts to his early years and course of education—"My father (he says) had me duly instructed in the Grammar School, *and by other* MASTERS *at home.* He then, after I had acquired a proficiency in various languages, and had made a considerable progress in philosophy, sent me to the University of Cambridge. Here I passed seven years in the usual course of instruction and study, with the approbation of the good, and free from any stain or imputation on my character; and also took my degree, as it is called, of Master of Arts, with approbation."[2]

Warton, the historian of English poetry, who, although free from the insane bigotry of Dr Samuel Johnson, had no liking to the Puritans, in his edition of Milton's Minor Poems, 1785, thus mentions Young:—

"Under such an instructor Milton probably first imbibed the principles of Puritanism; and, as a Puritan tutor was employed

[1] Todd's Milton, vol. i. p. 9.

[2] His own words may be quoted—"Pater me puerulum humaniorum literarum studiis destinavit; quas ita avide arripui, ut ab anno ætatis duodecimo vix unquam ante mediam noctem a lucubrationibus cubitum discederem; quæ prima oculorum pernicies fuit: quorum ad naturalem debilitatem accesserant et crebri capitis dolores; quæ omnia cum discendi impetum non retardarent, *et in ludo literario, et sub aliis domi Magistris erudiendum quotidie curavit:* ita variis instructum linguis, et percepta haud leviter philosophiæ dulcedine, ad Gymnasium gentis alterum, Cantabrigiam misit:" etc.—*Pro Populo Anglicano Defensio Secunda*, p. 82. Lond. 1654. 12mo.

to educate his son, we may fairly guess at the persuasions or inclinations of the father. . . . . The first and fourth of Milton's Familiar Epistles, both very respectful and affectionate, are to this Thomas Young. In the first, dated at London, *inter urbana diverticula*, March 26, 1625, he says he had resolved to send Young an epistle in verse, but thought proper, at the same time, to send in prose. The elegy now before us is this epistle in verse. In the second, dated from Cambridge, July 21, 1628, he says, " Rus tuum accersitus, simul ac ver adoleverit, libenter adveniam, ad capessendas anni, tuique non minus colloquii, delicias ; et ab urbano strepitu subducam me paulisper." Whatever were Young's religious instructions, our author professes to have received from this learned master his first introduction to the study of poetry, verse 29 :—

> Primus ego Aonios, illo praeeunte, recessus
> Lustrabam, et bifidi sacra vireta jugi ;
> Pieriosque hausi latices, Clióque favente,
> Castalio sparsi læta ter ora mero.

" Yet these couplets (Warton adds) may imply only a first acquaintance with the classics."

His Fourth Elegy, *Elegia Quarta, Anno ætatis* 18 (1627) is addressed,—

"Ad Thomam Junium praeceptorem suum, apud Mercatores Anglicos Hamburgæ agentes, Pastoris munere fungentem."

> Vivit ibi antiquæ clarus pietatis honore
> Præsul, Christicolas pascere doctus oves :
> Ille quidem est animæ plusquam pars altera nostræ :
> Dimidio vitæ vivere cogeo ego.

Another passage informs us that Young was then married :

> Invenies dulci cum conjuge forte sedentem.
> Mulcentem gremio pignora chara suo :
> Forsitan aut veterum prælarga volumina Patrum
> Versantem, aut veri Biblia sacra Dei.

Young (says Warton) " seems to have been driven back to England by the war in the Netherlands, not long after this elegy was written."

The first of Milton's letters addressed to Young has the date March 1625 : it apparently should be 1625–26, as the Fourth Elegy to which it refers was not likely to have been delayed for upwards of twelve months. This letter, in its literal translation,[1] is as follows :—

MILTON TO HIS TUTOR, THOMAS YOUNG.

" Though I had determined, my excellent tutor, to write you an epistle in verse, yet I could not satisfy myself without sending also another in prose, for the emotions of my gratitude, which your services so justly inspire, are too expansive and too warm to be expressed in the confined limits of poetical metre ; they demand the unconstrained freedom of prose, or rather the exuberant richness of Asiatic phraseology ; though it would far exceed my power accurately to describe how much I am obliged to you, even if I could drain dry all the sources of eloquence, or exhaust all the topics of discourse which Aristotle or the famed Parisian logician has collected. You complain with truth that my letters have been very few and very short ; but I do not grieve at the omission of so pleasurable a duty, so much as I rejoice at having such a place in your regard as makes you anxious often to hear from me. I beseech you not to take it amiss, that I have not now written to you for more than three years ; but with your usual benignity to impute it rather to circumstances than to inclination. For Heaven knows, that I regard you as a parent, that I have always treated you with the utmost respect, and that I was unwilling to tease you with my compositions. And I was anxious that, if my letters had nothing else to recommend them, they might be recommended by their rarity. And, lastly, since the ardour of my regard makes me imagine that you are always present, that I hear your voice and contemplate your looks ; and as thus (which is usually the case with lovers) I charm away my grief by the illusion of your presence, I was afraid when I wrote to you the idea of your distant separation should forcibly rush upon my mind, and that the pain of your absence, which was almost soothed into quiescence, should revive and disperse the

[1] I have availed myself of the translations in the excellent and convenient edition of Milton's Prose Works (Vol. III.), in Bohn's Standard Library.

pleasurable dream. I long since received your desirable present of the Hebrew Bible. I wrote this at my lodgings in the city, not, as usual, surrounded by my books. If, therefore, there be anything in this letter which either fails to give pleasure, or which frustrates expectation, it shall be compensated by a more elaborate composition as soon as I return to the dwelling of the muses.

"LONDON, *March* 26, 1625."

It is from Milton's Fourth Elegy, written in his eighteenth year, that we derive the information that the appointment which carried Young abroad was that of chaplain to the English Factory or Merchants, residing at Hamburgh.[1] It also shows that Young was then married, and had a family. Cowper, the English poet, has translated this Elegy with the other Latin verses by Milton. His version of the lines given by Warton in the above quotation, may be added, for the sake of their personal allusions.

ELEGY IV.

TO HIS TUTOR, THOMAS YOUNG, CHAPLAIN TO THE ENGLISH FACTORY AT HAMBURGH [1627].

Written in the Author's eighteenth year.

Hence my epistle—skim the deep—fly o'er
Yon smooth expanse to the Teutonic shore !
Haste, lest a friend should grieve for thy delay,
And the gods grant that nothing thwart thy way.

. . . . .

[1] It is now many long years ago since I first visited Hamburgh ; and being detained there by contrary winds for a few days, I remember having. at the English Chapel, made some vague and fruitless inquiries respecting Young. At that time I had no special object in view ; but some twenty years later, one of the resident merchants kindly renewed these inquiries, with no better success, as appears from the following :—

Extract from a note, dated in June 1842.—"Schiller wrote me some time ago that they had employed a person to search for the information you wanted, and at that time no light could be thrown upon it. Then subsequently wrote, ' we will not be able to give you any information regarding the English minister, as the archives have been destroyed by the late fire.' I am sorry that you are thus left as much in the dark as formerly."

The sands, that line the German coast, descried,
To opulent Hamburga turn aside!

.   .   .   .   .

There lives, deep learn'd and primitively just,
A faithful steward of his Christian trust,
My friend, and favourite inmate of my heart,
That now is forced to want its better part.

.   .   .   .   .

First led by him through sweet Aonian shade,
Each sacred haunt of Pindus I surveyed ;
And favour'd by the muse whom I implored,
Thrice on my lip the hallow'd stream I pour'd.
But thrice the sun's resplendent chariot roll'd
To Aries, has new-tinged his fleece with gold,
And Chloris twice has dress'd the meadows gay,
And twice has summer parch'd their bloom away,
Since last delighted on his looks I hung,
Or my ear drank the music of his tongue ;
Fly, therefore, and surpass the tempest's speed,
Aware thyself that there is urgent need !
Him, entering, thou shalt haply seated see
Beside his spouse, his infants on his knee
Or turning, page by page, with studious look,
Some bulky father, or God's holy book ;
Or ministering (which is his weightiest care)
To Christ's assembled flock their heavenly fare.
Give him, whatever his employment be,
Such gratulation as he claims, from me ;
And, with a downcast eye and carriage meek,
Addressing him, forget not thus to speak !
    If, compass'd round with arms, thou can'st attend
To verse, verse greets thee from a distant friend.

.   .   .   .   .

Works of William Cowper, by Southey, vol. x. pp. 187-189.

. According to the inscription on Young's monument, his appointment as Vicar of Stowmarket was in the year 1627 or 1628.
Milton's second letter to Young has the date July 21, 1628, after he was settled vicar of Stowmarket. The letter (in its translated form) may be added. That their friendly intercourse, by occasional visits to the Vicarage, as well as by correspondence, was maintained, need not be doubted.

10

Milton to Thomas Young.

" On reading your letter, my excellent Tutor, I find only one superfluous passage, an apology for not writing to me sooner ; for though nothing gives me more pleasure than to hear from you, how can I or ought I to expect that you should always have leisure enough from more serious and more sacred engagements to write me, particularly when it is kindness, and not duty, which prompts you to write? Your many recent services must prevent me from entertaining any suspicion of your forgetfulness or neglect. Nor do I see how you could possibly forget one on whom you had conferred so many favours. Having an invitation into your part of the country in the spring, I shall readily accept it, that I may enjoy the deliciousness of the season as well as that of your conversation ; and that I may withdraw myself for a short time from the tumult of the city to your rural mansion, as to the renowned portico of Zeno or Tusculan of Tully, where you live on your little farm, with a moderate fortune, but a princely mind ; and where you practise the contempt, and triumph over the temptations of ambition, pomp, luxury, and all that follows the chariot of fortune, or attracts the gaze and admiration of the thoughtless multitude. I hope that you, who deprecated the blame of delay, will pardon me for my precipitance ; for after deferring this letter to the last, I chose rather to write a few lines, however deficient in elegance, than to say nothing at all.—Adieu, reverend Sir.

" Cambridge, July 21, 1628."

That Young and other Puritan ministers may afterwards have found it prudent to leave their livings, during Archbishop's Laud's ascendency and the existence of the Star Chamber, is not improbable, as at least he seems to have been absent from Stowmarket in the years 1638 and 1639. At that time he published anonymously his learned work on the observance of the Christian Sabbath, the DIES DOMINICA, &c., 1639, 4to.[1] It has no place or printer's name.

[1] When last in the great mercantile city of Hamburgh, I took the opportunity of examining the books in the Public Library, and came upon a copy of Young's *Dies Dominica*, 1639. It had no inscription,

but was evidently printed abroad. In the prefatory address to "the Orthodox Church of Christ," he says the work was written "to benefit chiefly thy natural sons that sojourn *in Germany, which I love upon many accounts.*" This, indeed, may allude to the earlier period of his life. I have a presentation copy to Nathanael Bacon, the words indicating enigmatically the initials of the author's name, T. and Y. (the letter of Pythagoras) :--

" Post Tau, Pythagoræ littere scripta docet."

Milton, after his mother's death, was allowed to visit the Continent in 1637. He returned about August 1639, when the King's second expedition against the Scots was defeated by General Lesley. In his youthful ardour for civil and religious liberty, he tells us that he shortened his travels abroad, and laid aside for a time his lofty aspirations, that he might join in the religious strife which prevailed in regard to Episcopal authority, and the Reformation of the Church in discipline as well as government. That he was to some extent influenced by the sentiments of his old preceptor may be taken for granted.

In the year 1640 Joseph Hall, Bishop of Norwich, published anonymously " An Humble Remonstrance to the High Court of Parliament." This manifesto gave rise to a learned controversy in regard to Episcopal claims of antiquity, and matters connected with Prelatic Church government. One of his opponents was Thomas Young, who, along with other four ministers, produced a joint Answer to the Remonstrance under the name of SMECTYMNVVS,

and was indeed entered in the catalogue as the work of an unknown author. I was shown a biographical article on Thomas Young, by that eminent German historian, the late Dr J. M. Lappenberg, who was then Keeper of the Records, but was much disappointed to find that it furnished no local information regarding Young, as might have been expected from the *Archivarius.* It contains little else than the notice derived from Milton's Elegy. The collection in which this article appears is entitled " Zeitschrift des Vereines für Hamburgische Geschichte. Erster Band." Hamburg, 1841. 8vo. " Art. xxix. Thomas Young, Cappellan der Court der *Merchant-Adventurers* zu Hamburg. Von Herrn Dr J. M. Lappenberg."—P. 309.

I wish, however, I had been aware of this article when the Author made his last visit to Scotland.

in 1641. This name was assumed from the initial letters of the live divines engaged in writing it—namely, **Stephen Marshall, Edward Calamy, Thomas Young, Matthew Newcommen,** and **William Spurstow.** One circumstance which has rendered this controversy more memorable is the prominent share taken by Milton in its progress, and which requires more than a passing allusion. The Answer which produced Bishop Hall's Defence of the Humble Remonstrance, was followed by A Vindication of the Answer, and this by A Short Answer to the tedious Vindication —all in 1641. It was about this stage of the controversy that Milton came forward, like a knight-errant, in defence of Smectymnuus, as may be seen from the list of tracts on this controversy, given in the Appendix, (See p. 17.)

At the General Assembly held at Edinburgh, in July 1641, Alexander Henderson, Moderator, in a speech, as reported by Baillie, " Advysed the Towne of Edinburgh, and other prime Burrowes, to intertain abroad some good spirits, who might be their owne, if they proved apt for their service. Also he shew the expediencie of calling home one Mr Thomas Young from England, the author of *Dies Dominica*, and of the *Smectymnuus* for the most part; and of Mr Colvine from Sedan, to whose commendation he spake much," &c. (vol. i. p. 366).

In 1643 Thomas Young was nominated a member of the Assembly of Divines at Westminster. Both Lightfoot and Baillie make mention of his occasional speeches on points in discussion. Baillie also says he was one of those who reasoned for the divine institution of the office of Ruling elder, and had likewise an active hand in preparing the portion of the Directory, for reading of the Scriptures and singing of Psalms.[1] At this time Herbert Palmer having been removed from the church of Duke's Place, London, to the new Church at Westminster, Young received a call to become his successor. In the year following, by an ordinance of Parliament, the Earl of Manchester held a visitation for the reformation of the University of Cambridge; and, in virtue of that authority, he ejected "for gross scandalls," the heads of five

---

[1] These reports are confirmed by the MS. Proceedings of the Westminster Assembly of Divines.—See APPENDIX.

colleges; and, as Baillie says (vol. ii. page 148), he wrote to the Westminster Assembly he had "made choise of five of our number to be Masters in their places—Messrs Palmer, Vines, Seaman, Arrowsmith, and our countryman Young, requiring the Assembly's approbation of his choise; which was unanimously given, for they are all very good and able divines." Young's place was to be Master of Jesus College, in the room of Dr Richard Sterne, who was ejected; and the Earl of Manchester came in person to the College Chapel, and there, with some formalities, placed him in the chair as Master, on the 12th April 1644.

Young is said to have been concerned in printing a small tract or remonstrance against the Engagement, under the title of "The Humble Proposals of sundry Learned and Pious Divines within this Kingdom, concerning the Engagement intended to be imposed on them for their Subscription." Lond. 1649. 4to. The copy I have, and others dated 1650, give no indication of the writer.

This Remonstrance had no effect; and, as one of those who felt themselves constrained to refuse to sign the Engagement in 1650, Young was deprived of his Mastership at Cambridge. It would seem, indeed, that he was no enemy to pluralities, as his connexion with Stowmarket still existed, by his employing a curate, and probably giving him the use of the vicarage.

We may presume, therefore, that Dr Young, on the termination of what we may call his public career during the Commonwealth, lived in retirement, in the midst of his parish, until his death, which took place on the 28th November 1655, in the 68th year of his age. He was interred within the parish church of which he had been Vicar (with some interruptions), for the space of twenty-eight years. The parish register simply states—" Dr Younge, clerke, was buried the first day of December 1655."

From the same register we learn that his wife predeceased him :—" Mrs Rebecca Young, the wife of Dr Young, clerke, was buried the 25th day of April 1651."

As an author, Young's writings are not numerous. Besides his share in the Smectymnuus controversy, we have only one printed sermon by him, preached before the House of Commons on a

14

fast day, " Hope's Encouragement."[1] The dedication is signed,
"Tho. Young, S. Evangelii in Comitatu Suffolciensi, Minister."
His *Dies Dominica* was highly commended by several of his contemporaries, and a translation of it published, with a preface by
Richard Baxter, London, 1672, small 8vo. The translator's name
is not mentioned, any more than that of the author, who is
styled "a man eminent in his time for great learning, judgment,
piety, humility, but especially for his acquaintance with the
writings of the ancient teachers of the Churches, and the doctrine
and practise of former ages." In his own work, "The Divine
Appointment of the Lord's Day Proved," &c., London, 1671,
Baxter specially mentions, " Dr Young, in his *Dies Dominica*,
under the name of Theophilus Loncardiensis," &c. " But again,
I must give notice that Dr T. Young's *Dies Dominica* is the
book which I agree with in the method and middle way of deter-
mining this controversy."

Edward Leigh of Oxford, in Book V. " Of such as were famous
for zeal in the True Religion, or in Learning," enumerates[2]:—

" Dr Thomas Young, a member of the Assembly of Divines,
and a learned divine. One very well versed in the Fathers. He
was the author of that excellent treatise entitled *Dies Dominica*,
and one of those five that made SMECTYMNUUS."

Robert Baillie, in a letter, dated December 31, 1655, to the
Rev. Simon Ashe, minister at London, in referring to various
literary matters, and to the sermons of Mr Stephen Marshall
then "a-dying," adds,—"I hear Dr Young has a good Treatise
for the presse." Ashe, in his reply, after noticing the death of
Marshall, says,—" Dr Young is dead also ; and his papers about
Discipline are so voluminous, that no stationer will undertake to
print them, because that controversie lyeth dead among us, and
few inquire for any books of that subject."[3]

No trace has been discovered of such books or papers as still
existing.

1 The Sermon preached at the last Solemn Fast before the House of
Commons, 28th February 1644, was, as usual, printed by an order of the
House. It is entitled, " Hope's Encouragement," on the text Psalm xxxi.
24. London, 1644. 4to. pp. iv. 38.

2 A Treatise of Religion and Learning. p. 369. Lond. 1656. Folio.

3 Letters and Journals, vol. iii. pp. 305. 306.

The appearance in a local history of a detailed account of Young furnishes us with more precise information, on some points of his history. The work referred to is "The History of Stowmarket, the ancient county town of Suffolk, &c. By the Rev. A. G. H. Hollingsworth, M.A., Rural Dean and Vicar of Stowmarket with Stowupland." Ipswich, 1844. Small 4to.

In this volume chapter xxviii. is entitled, "The Life of the Rev. Dr Young, Vicar of Stowmarket, from 1628 to 1655, and tutor of Milton the Poet" (pp. 187–194), with views of the Church, the Vicarage, and of Milton's mulberry tree.

Mr Hollingsworth, like other writers, misled by Aubrey's erroneous notions,[1] says,—"Where Dr Young was born is uncertain," and supposes that he was a native of Essex.[2] "In 1623 his tutorship of Milton must have terminated, for the latter was admitted a pensioner at Cambridge on the 12th February 1624.

"On the 27th of March 1628, Mr Thomas Younge was instituted to the united vicarages of St Peter and St Mary, in Stowe, on the presentation of Mr John Howe, a gentleman then residing in the town, and a man of wealth, whose ancestors had been great cloth manufacturers in this place and neighbourhood. The living was worth L.300 per annum, which was considerable preferment in those times, and equal to L.600 a year now."—Page 187.

"In 1628 we have seen him instituted to these livings, and he (Young) must have remained generally in constant residence, because we possess his signature to the vestry accounts, in a curious quarto book, which contains the annual expenses of Stowupland parish for eighty-four years. At the parish meetings, and at the audit of each year's accounts, Vicar Young presided, with some

---

[1] I think it obvious that Aubrey's words—"his Schoolmaster there was Thomas Young, a Puritan in Essex, who cutt his haire short," apply to Milton's "clustering locks," and not to Young himself, as usually supposed.

[2] PROFESSOR MASSON, in his elaborate and valuable Life of Milton, vol. i., 1859, in giving an account of Thomas Young as one of Milton's tutors, was quick enough sighted to detect in his Latin designation *Loncardiensis* a clue to Young's early history, of which no distinct public notice had previously been given.

exceptions, from the year 1629 to 1655, and his autograph is attested to each page.‡"

(In a foot note is added the actual dates of his signature, "‡ Thomas Young, 1629, April 7—1630, April 11—1631, April 23—1633—1634—1636—1637—1652—1655, April 17.")

"Dr Young, therefore, kept a curate during this period (1643 to 1653). His signature does not appear attached to the vestry accounts, but the signatures of various persons who I presume are his substitutes; and thus his visits to Stowmarket, though annual, were probably during summer. What more likely," Mr Hollingsworth adds, "than that Milton should have often come down to obtain the refreshing pleasures of conversation with his old tutor?"—Page 193.

In regard to Milton he says—"From the long connexion of Dr Young with the parish, and his continued residence here, it is not unlikely that several, if not many visits, extending over a period of nearly thirty years whilst his tutor held the living, were made by the Poet to this place. Tradition has constantly connected his name with the mulberry trees of the vicarage, which he planted; but of those one only remains. This venerable relic of the past is much decayed, and is still (1844) in vigorous bearing, although many limbs have fallen from its trunk."—Page 188.

" How often did the poet Milton sit in these rooms and visit this old vicarage? is a question which must occur to every one who peruses the preceding outline of Dr Young's employments and connections. The Vicar was married, and therefore could command more of the comforts of home than a solitary bachelor. His wife did not die till April 1651. . . . I believe that the Poet must have held very frequent intercourse with the Vicar, and may have been often in Stowmarket."—Page 193.

" When Dr Young died, his epitaph was inscribed with some care by a friendly hand, and an unwilling admission is made of the opposition he had encountered. It is now illegible, and some of its lines appear to have been carefully erased. But the following copy is taken from one made many years since, when the epitaph was fresh and legible. He lies on the right and in front of the reading-desk in the middle aisle.

Requiescat in pace."

[Dr Young's Epitaph.]

Here is committed to earth's trust,
Wise, pious, spotlesse, learned dust ;
Who living more adorned the place,
Than the place him, such was God's grace.

To
Thos. Younge.
D.D.
Mem. of Je. Coll. Cam.
A member of ye late Assem.
Pastor here An. 28.
Died An. Ætatis 68.
Xti. 1655.
Nov. 28.

Who, with his deare wife and eldest
son Tho. Young, M.A., and President
of Je. Coll. Camb. lyes here, expect-
ing yᵉ Resurrection.

Mr Hollingsworth adds :—"Is the verse of this epitaph from Milton's pen or not? The probability is quite in favour that the pupil should write the last memorial of one whom he so highly honoured and loved as his old master. Nor is the verse itself, with the exception of the last line, unlike the character of Milton ; and this last may have been mutilated, and rendered inharmonious by the stone-cutter, who has also confused the death of the father and son."—Page 194.

" His (Young) learning was profound, and, from the character of his mind, became severe and polemical. He wrote not so much as a disciple of truth without prejudice, as of truth with a party. . . . . To judge of him by his scanty remains, we must pro-nounce him, like his pupil, John Milton, a republican in politics, and a Calvinistic dogmatist in theology."—Page 187.

" His portrait at the Vicarage possesses the solemn faded yellow-ness of a man given to much austere meditation ; yet there is sufficient energy in the eye and mouth to show, as he is preaching in Geneva gown and bands, with a little Testament in hand, that he is a man who could both write and speak and think with great vigour."—Page 188.

B

It might be easy to quote several incidental notices of the estimation in which Young's personal character was held by his contemporaries. I shall only mention two. One, the Rev. Samuel Clarke, in his account of Herbert Palmer's translation from Duke's Place, London (see p. 12), says that Palmer, unwilling to leave his flock destitute of an able, faithful pastor, "prevailed with Master Thomas Young (since Doctor in Divinity and Master of Jesus Colledge in Cambridge) to succeed him there ; who was also an eminent member of the Assembly of Divines, A MAN OF GREAT LEARNING, OF MUCH PRUDENCE AND PIETY, AND OF GREAT ABILITY AND FIDELITY IN THE WORK OF THE MINISTRY."[1] The other, the Ejected Rectors of two neighbouring parishes, in 1674, speak of him as "THAT REVEREND, LEARNED, ORTHODOX, PRUDENT, AND HOLY MAN, DR YOUNG."[2]

[1] Clarke's Lives of Thirty-Two English Divines. Third edition, (p. 194.) Lond. 1677. folio.

[2] Prefatory letters to a posthumous volume of Sermons bearing this title " JEHOVAH JIREH; or the Saints' Relief in Time of Exigency, held forth in several Sermons preached at Stowmarket, in Suffolk, by Samuel Blackerby, Minister of the Gospel and Vicar there. London, printed for Nevill Simons, 1674." 8vo.

Mr Hollingsworth, to whom we are indebted for an account of the book, copies the Author's address to his dear Parishioners, dated in December 1673. Blackerby, who died and was buried in Stowmarket Church, 21st December 1674, had been Curate after Dr Young's incumbency, and for ten years had presided as Vicar in the parish.

The following is a facsimile of Young's signature in 1633 and in 1655, dated Stowupland, from the MS. volume of Vestry Accounts, mentioned above, p. 16 :—

POSTSCRIPT AND APPENDIX.

Finding that I could not be present at the earlier Meetings of the Institute held last year at Bury St Edmunds, the immediate object in printing these pages was relinquished. I gladly, however, availed myself of the opportunity, when the meetings had closed, to devote a day for visiting Stowmarket; and I now subjoin a few particulars on the following points:—

    I. *The Portrait of Dr Young.*

    II. *The Church in which he was interred ; and*

    III. *The Vicarage House, with which Milton's name has traditionally been associated.*

The delay in completing this Tract has also enabled me to revise it carefully, and to add two or three other Notes, along with a full and accurate List of Tracts connected with the Smectymnuus Controversy.

D. L.

Edinburgh, *November* 1870.

I.

Portrait of Dr Thomas Young.

The circular sent to Members of the Archæological Institute respecting the Annual Congress to be held in July 1869 at Bury St Edmunds, announced a proposed Exhibition of Portraits of eminent persons connected with the county of Suffolk. I was thus led to call the attention of Edmund M. Dewing, Esq., the Honorary Local Secretary, to the Portrait described by Mr Hollingsworth (see p. 17) as preserved in the Vicarage House, Stowmarket. Although it was found necessary to postpone the intended Portrait Exhibition, I was glad to find that an application had been made, with success, to the proprietor for the Portrait of Young, and thus I had a favourable opportunity of examining it at leisure. The old volume of Vestry Accounts, containing his signature as Vicar (see p. 18), was also among the articles of local interest collected in the temporary Museum.

Being satisfied of the genuineness of the Portrait, I thought it worth being at the expense of having it cut in wood by a London artist, employed by the Institute. For this purpose two small photographs were taken, but they were somewhat indistinct, owing to the state of the painting. When the cut was finished in a very excellent style, it nevertheless, to my regret, would not serve my purpose, inasmuch as, from one cause or other, it could not be called a portrait of Dr Thomas Young. Various attempts by a different process were tried in Edinburgh, but not having the advantage of recourse to the original, one and all of them were equally unsatisfactory. Yet not wishing to be disappointed in giving some likeness, a last attempt was made, by the aid of photo-zincography, to transfer to stone an exact copy of the small photograph, and I am glad to think that the Portrait prefixed to this tract serves at least to convey a tolerable idea of the character and expression of the original.

In the reign of Charles the First, the inhabitants of the parish, like most parts of the kingdom, were divided into royalists and parliamentary adherents. It is not necessary to say to which party "the puritanical Vicar," as Mr Hollingsworth calls him, belonged ; but in mentioning the name of William Manning, he adds :— "*From whose descendants I obtained the portrait of Dr Young,* which, though faded, is still in good preservation" (p. 158, note). The portrait is what is called a head-size, painted on canvas, but now in rather poor condition. Upon Mr Hollingsworth's death,[1] it came into the possession of his son-in-law, H. C. Mathew, Esq., Felixstow, near Ipswich ; and this gentleman responded to the application by obligingly lending it for the proposed Exhibition. As the work of an unknown artist, without either inscription or date, it loses much of the interest that might attach to it, had it remained an heir-loom in the Vicarage house at Stowmarket.

[1] The Rev. Arthur George Harper Hollingsworth, M.A., Vicar and Patron of Stowmarket, Suffolk, Dean Rural of Stow, died at Felixstow, Suffolk, aged 56, on the 2d of January 1859.—*Gentleman's Magazine*, p. 215.

II.

THE CHURCH OF STOWMARKET.

Stowmarket is situated in the centre of the county of Suffolk, 12 miles from Ipswich, and 81 N.E. from London. The church, which is dedicated to St Peter and St Mary, is a spacious and handsome edifice of the fifteenth century, with a square tower, and, like several of the East Anglian churches, surmounted by a slender spire of wood rising to the height of 120 feet.[1] Mr Hollingsworth has given two views of the church, exterior and interior. It also appears in his view of the Vicarage, with Milton's mulberry tree.

In visiting the Church, my chief object was to see the monument,[2] or rather the inscription, on a marble stone, over the place where Young was interred. This was pointed out to me by the parish clerk (Mr E. Barnard), for without his obliging aid I could not have discovered it, being in the centre passage, between the pews, which is covered with matting. It is a large horizontal slab, of 5 feet 7 inches in length, by 2 feet in breadth.

Mr Hollingsworth, in referring to the inscription (see p. 16), says :—" It is now illegible, and some of its lines appear to have been carefully erased." The inscription corresponds exactly with that printed at page 17, and having this in my hand, I found no difficulty in tracing all the lines. There is, indeed, at the top a blank space, apparently neither mutilated nor effaced, but left unfinished for some ornament, a shield of arms, or perhaps a medallion head.

III.

THE VICARAGE HOUSE.

On leaving the Church, I was conducted to the Vicarage, and although an entire stranger, on explaining the object of my visit, I was most kindly received by the present incumbent, the Rev. HENRY LEWIS. In the " History of Stowmarket," in 1844,

---

[1] Topographical Dictionary of England, by Samuel Lewis, vol. iv.

[2] It is called "a monument." in the " Beauties of England and Wales:" Suffolk, vol. xiv. p. 205.

one of the views, already mentioned, represents the Vicarage, and Milton's mulberry tree, so long associated with the name of the poet. Of this view an accurate copy, somewhat reduced to suit the size of the present tract, is given on a separate leaf. The late Mr Hollingsworth subsequently made a large addition to the house of two public rooms ; but the interior remains very much in its original state,—one of the bed-rooms being assigned, by tradition, as Milton's during his occasional visits to his old tutor. The house is in a pleasant situation, but is not improved by the manufactories which have recently been erected in its neighbourhood.

I regret much now to learn that these old cherished associations have in a great measure ceased. " Owing to the dilapidated state into which the old Vicarage House, from the lapse of time, had fallen, and from which it could not be recovered so as to retain any of its original features, it has been recently exchanged for another house in the town better situated and more adapted for the Vicar's residence. It is hoped the Mulberry Tree will still be preserved."

IV.

LONCARDY AND REDGORTON.

Loncardy or Luncarty, in the parish of Redgorton, has an historical memory as mentioned in the note to p. 4. In modern times it is noted chiefly for its extensive linen-cloth bleachfields.

Owing to the imperfect state of the Registers at that early time, I have not been enabled to ascertain what family William Young, minister of these united parishes, left; and it is unnecessary to indulge in conjecture. He acted as Clerk to the Presbytery of Perth. In the year 1620, being then " an aged and infirm man," the minutes record some proceedings regarding a dastardly attempt made on him by one of his parishioners, for acting by direction of the Presbytery in a case of discipline. (See extract, " Statistical Account, Perthshire," p. 178.) Young appears from the Presbytery records to have died between 25th April and 30th November 1625.

William Crookshank, Young's son-in-law and successor, as minister of Redgorton, was ordained by Alexander Lyndsay.

Bishop of Dunkeld, before 8th February 1626. He joined the Protesters in 1651, but was overlooked at the Restoration. Fasti Eccl. Scot., by the Rev. Dr Hew Scott, vol. ii. p. 655).

V.

THE ENGLISH CHURCH AT HAMBURGH.

Among the various churches in the city of Hamburgh before the destructive fire of 1842, there was an English Episcopal Chapel, a plain building of comparatively modern erection; having, I imagine, no connexion with the factory of " the English Merchant Adventurers," which in 1623 was established in that great emporium of foreign commerce, in the duchy of Holstein, situated on the north bank of the river Elbe.

There is a rare volume of " Songs of Sion," by William Loe, " printed at Hamborough," in 1620. The author was for a time Chaplain to the English Factory at Hamburgh, and the several divisions of his work are dedicated to the leading English merchants there. He preached a sermon before the King at Whitehall in 1622, so probably he had then resigned his charge, and returned to England. We may therefore safely conclude that he was Young's immediate predecessor. According to Anthony Wood, Loe was one of the Prebendaries of Gloucester, and obtained the degree of Doctor of Divinity. (Athenæ Oxon., by Bliss, vol. iii. p. 183.)

The Rev. John Wing had been chaplain previously for some years. In June 1620 he was settled as Minister of the English Church of Flushing, where he published the following Sermons which he had preached at Hamburgh.

1. " Jacob's Staffe to beare up the Faithful, and to beate down the Profane. Formerly preached at Hamburgh by John Wing, late pastor to the English Church there, as his farewell to the famous fellowship of Merchant Adventurers of England, resident in that city. And now published and dedicated, to the honour and use of that most worthy Society, there, or wheresoever being." Flushing, 1621. 4to, pp. 216.

2. " Abel's Offering; a Sermon preached at Hamburg in November 1617, and now published at the instant entreaty of a godly

Christian. By John Wing, (then) Pastor to the English Church there." Flushing, 1621. 4to, pp. 71.

Wing was translated from Flushing to the Hague in May 1627. (Rev. Dr Steven's " History of the Scottish Church, Rotterdam," pp. 302, 306, 308. Edinburgh, 1833. 8vo.)

VI.

Dr Young's "Dies Dominica."

Of this work, printed abroad in 1639, there is here given on a separate leaf a facsimile of the ornamented title-page, and of the Author's autograph inscription on the copy (which has MS. corrections in his own hand) presented to Nathaniel Bacon (see p. 11). The border vignettes, cut in wood, are remarkably well designed ; if the place of printing had been ascertained, we might perhaps have guessed the name of the artist. It is followed by a printed title, which reads as follows :—

"Dies Dominica, sive Succincta narratio ex S. Scripturarum, & venerandæ antiquitatis Patrum testimoniis concinnata, et Duobus Libris distincta: Quorum Priori, diei Dominicæ observationem ab ipsis Apostolis, Ecclesiaque Christiana continua serie solennem fuisse habitam, ejus institutionem fuisse divinam, & quæ ejus solennitatem impediant, declaratur : Posteriori vero in quibus ejus sanctificatio consistat ostenditur. In quibus etiam, Variæ Ecclesiasticæ antiquitates cognitu non indignæ explicantur," Anno 1639. 4to, 12 leaves and pp. 132, printed in a small type.

The Epistola Dedicatoria is addressed—

" Sanctissimæ, Orthodoxæ Christi Ecclesiæ, à fœdissimis Pontificiorum sordibus feliciter repurgatæ, Matri charissimæ, Gratiam, et Pacem."

It ends with the following sentence—

" Habes itaque (MATER DILECTISSIMA) in hoc opusculo emittendo animi mei propositum. *Tu* igitur, quâ es in *Tuos* humanitate, σφάλματα quanta quanta sint in hisce congerendis condonabis, & ingenioli mei tenuitatem, germanis T. Filiis in Germania (mihi pluribus nominibus colenda) præcipuè commorantibus pro-

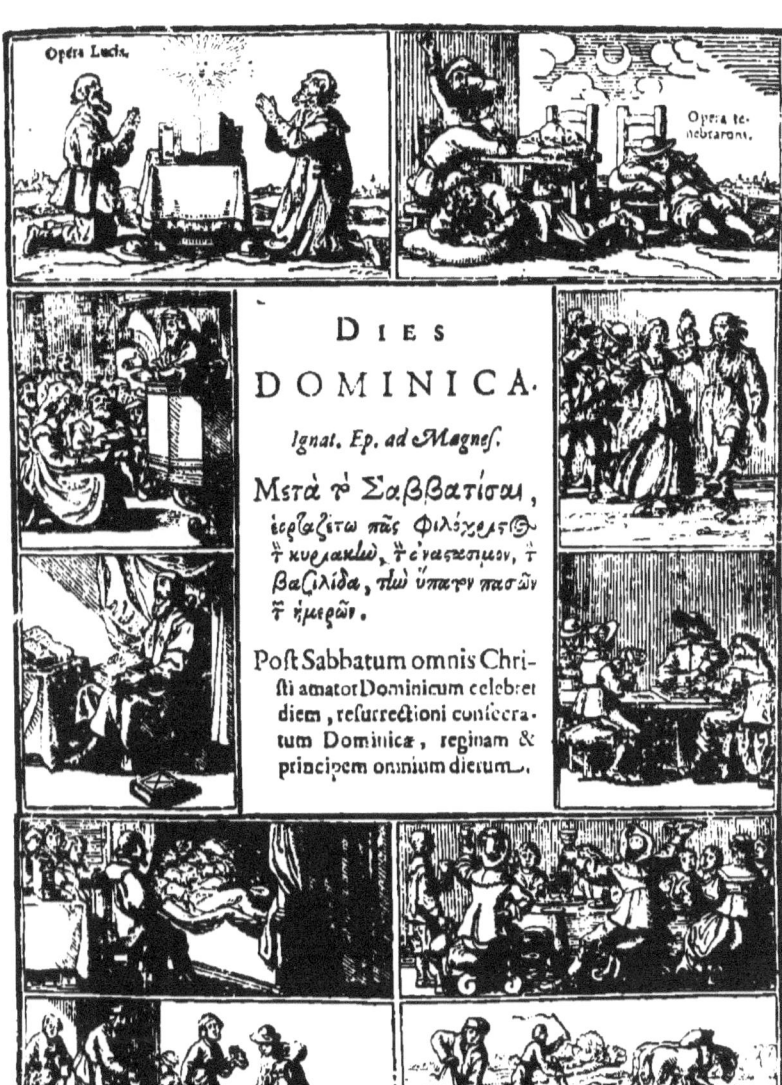

Opera Lucis.

Opera tenebrarum.

DIES DOMINICA.

Ignat. Ep. ad Magnes.

Μετὰ τὸ Σαββατίσαι, ἐργαζέτω πᾶς φιλόχριστος τ̄ κυριακὴ, τ̄ ἀναστάσιμον, τ̄ βασιλίδα, τ̄ ὑπατον πασῶν τ̄ ἡμερῶν.

Post Sabbatum omnis Christi amator Dominicum celebret diem, resurrectioni consecratum Dominicæ, reginam & principem omnium dierum.

Clariss. antiquæ Nobilitatis V.
D. Nathan. Baroni armigeri,

hæc Testimona de Dominica solennitate,

non fuco dealbata, nec fide Hellenistica veritata, vera
simplicitate, non falso nominata Columbina depromita e
ss. Patrum sinceritatis; nuß per ferrea latera contra omnem
Ecclesiastica Historia veritatem supportata; sed ipsissimis
ss. Patrum verbis, ferendum genuinum ipsorum sensum, prout
habet: Quæ ad buldinam veritatem, illum instar vernalis
rosæ migrescent, an modestum candidi, et nullo prejudicio
præoccupati Lectoris examen patientur
limatiss. Judicio relinquit,
qui Ei
L. M.

D iis cujus nomen discrimine festa,
Post Tau, Pythagoræ littera scripta docet.

desse pro virili conantem, æqui bonique consules : hoc demisse
petit, qui

Te, Tuosque, sincero amore in Christo colit,

THEOPHILUS PHILO—KURIACES

Loncardiensis."

The English translation on the first leaf has "DIES DOMINICA,
OR THE LORD'S DAY." The next leaf has the full title—
"THE LORDS DAY, Or, a succinct Narration compiled out of
the Testimonies of H. SCRIPTURE, and the Reverend Ancient
FATHERS : and divided into Two Books. In the former whereof
is declared That the observation of the Lords Day was from the
Apostles ; and by the Christian Church solemnized in a continual
series : that its Institution was Divine; and what things do
hinder its solemnity. In the Later is shewn, In what things its
Sanctification doth consist. In both which also Several Ecclesiastical Antiquities, not unworthy to be known, are explained,
and Lately Translated out of the Latine. London, printed by E.
Leach, 1672." Small 8vo, 28 leaves and pp. 412.

The address To the Reader, by Richard Baxter, is dated Sept.
2, 1671. He says,—"I take this Book to be of singular weight
and worth ; which having declared in my own, lately published,
on this subject, it hath occasioned many to enquire after it ; and a
worthy Knight, who had this translation by him, to be willing to
publish it." . . .

The Epistle Dedicatory "To the Holy, Orthodox Church of
Christ, happily cleansed from the filth of Popery, My dear Mother,
Grace and Peace ;" has the original signature

"Theophilus Philo-kuriaces Loncardiensis."

Of recent authors who have specially noticed Young's *Dies
Dominica,* may be enumerated, Professor Masson, "Life of Milton," vol. i., 185 ; the Rev. James Gilfillan, "The Sabbath,"
1861 ; and Robert Cox, Esq., "Literature of the Sabbath Question," 2 vols., 1865.

VII.

SMECTYMNUUS AND MILTON.

In 1612 King James succeeded by various means, by bribery
and corruption, and banishment of the most resolute opposers,

in at length imposing a form of Episcopal government on the Scottish Church. The persistent attempts of Charles the First, in 1637, to have the forms of worship changed by the introduction of a Liturgy or Book of Common Prayer (in some parts resembling the Romish service), alarmed and excited the religious feelings of the people against Prelacy. A scheme was then devised and acted upon, which proved most effectual in thwarting these and other innovations contemplated by the King and his priestly advisers. This was the renewal of the National Confession of 1580, with such additions "as the change of tyme and the present occasion requyred." The first day of March 1638 is memorable in history by the scene in the Greyfriars' Churchyard, when this Confession or Solemn engagement was sworn with uplifted hands, and subscribed by persons of all degrees, nobility, gentry, burgesses, ministers, and others, assembled from different parts of Scotland. Copies of this memorable deed, carefully written on parchment, having at the head of each the signatures of the leading Covenanters, were transmitted to all the principal towns and parishes for additional signatures; and thus obtained the adherence of nearly the entire population throughout the length and breadth of the land. (See Lists of such MSS. in the Proceedings of the Antiquaries of Scotland, vol. iv., p. 238). A free General Assembly was deemed essential, in order to have such matters discussed and settled. This memorable Assembly was held at Glasgow in November 1638, when Presbytery was firmly re-established, the Bishops deposed, and Diocesan Episcopacy in all its forms, root and branches, overthrown and abjured. This great movement has been termed the Second Reformation.

In England, the Parliament which met in November 1640, by granting liberty of the Press, and freedom of debate, proved no less fatal to the King's despotic measures. At this time, when dissent prevailed, the high pretensions of the Hierarchy, and its Divine right, as transmitted by direct and uninterrupted Apostolical succession, were boldly impugned. One of the ablest and most zealous defenders of Episcopacy was Dr Joseph Hall, then Bishop of Exeter, and afterwards of Norwich. His first tract was " Episcopacy by Divine Right Asserted, in Three Parts." London,

1640, 4to. In this work he maintained the doctrine " that Prelatic Superiority is not only a holy and lawful, but a divine Institution;" and also asserted, that " the Presbyterian government hath no true footing, either in Scripture or the practice of the Church in all ages from Christ's time to the present."

In the same year Bishop Hall, under the designation of "a dutifull sonne of the Church," published " An Humble Remonstrance to the High Court of Parliament." His object was to make " a too just complaint of the shamefull number of Libels, lately dropped from our lawlesse presses." It drew forth the learned Answer under the name of SMECTYMNUUS, which was recognised as the joint production of five Puritan divines, the word adopted as an anagram consisting of the initial letters of their names. Of this Answer, Bishop Hall says, " My single Remonstrance is encountred with a plurall Adversary that talks in the style of *We* and *Us*: Their names, persons, qualities, numbers, I care not to know." On the title-page, as their Answer is divided into Five Parts, we might have conjectured that each of the writers had prepared one of these divisions. There is, however, nothing in the tract itself to warrant the conjecture. The impression which this tract produced was no doubt great, by establishing the grounds of Presbyterian church government in opposition to the high exclusive claims of Prelacy. According to Baillie, the chief author of this tract was Young, and this may have had some effect on the mind of his pupil, the great English poet, who engaged so keenly in this controversy. Bishop Hall rejoined in " A Defence of the Humble Remonstrance." This produced " A Vindication of the Answer," by the same Smectymnuus, on the one side, and " A Short Answer of the tedious Vindication of Smectymnuus," on the other.

It does not appear that Milton on his return to England in 1639 took any immediate share in the controversies which engaged so much public attention. In his Second Defence of the People of England (1652), he gives the following statement regarding his share in these polemical disputes :—

" The vigour of the Parliament had begun to humble the pride of the Bishops. As long as the liberty of speech was no longer subject to control, all mouths began to be opened against the bishops; some complained of the vices of the individuals, others of those of the order. They said it was unjust that they alone should differ from the model of other Reformed churches; that the Government of the church should be according to the pattern of other churches, and particularly the Word of God. This awakened all my attention and my zeal. I saw that a way was opening for the establishment of real liberty; that the foundation was laying for the deliverance of man from the yoke of slavery and superstition; that the principles of religion, which were the first objects of our care, would exert a salutary influence on the manners and constitution of the republic; and as I had from my youth studied the distinctions between religious and civil rights, I perceived that if I ever wished to be of use, I ought at least not to be wanting to my country, to the Church, and to many of my fellow-Christians, in a crisis of so much danger; I therefore determined to relinquish the other pursuits in which I was engaged, and to transfer the whole force of my talents and my industry to this one important object. I accordingly wrote two books to a friend concerning the Reformation of the Church of England. Afterwards, when two Bishops of superior distinction vindicated their privileges against some principal Ministers, I thought that on those topics, to the consideration of which I was led solely by my love of truth, and my reverence for Christianity, I should not probably write worse than those who were contending only for their emoluments and usurpations. I therefore answered the one in two books, of which the first is inscribed, Concerning Prelatical Episcopacy, and the other, Concerning the Mode of Ecclesiastical Government; and I replied to the other in some Animadversions, and soon after in an Apology. On this occasion it was supposed that I brought a timely succour to the Ministers, who were hardly a match for the eloquence of their opponents, and from that time I was actively employed in refuting any answers that appeared. When the Bishops could no longer resist the multitude of their assailants, I had leisure to turn my thoughts to other subjects; to the promotion of real and substantial liberty; which is rather to be sought from within than from without; and whose existence depends not so much on the terror of the sword, as on sobriety of conduct and integrity of life."[1]

It has been customary to cry up the superior learning of the Episcopalian controversialists at the expense of the Smectymnuans, and Milton himself, in the above passage, with some self-glorification, assumes that they stood in need of his assistance in contending with such learned Prelates as Hall and Ussher; but hear his own explicit statement on this head, at the time, in his Apology, published in 1642.

"And here let me have pardon, Readers, if the remembrance of that which he [the Remonstrant] hath licenc't himselfe to utter contemptuously of those Reverend men, provoke me to doe that over againe, which some expect I should excuse as too freely done; since I have two provocations, his latest insulting in his Short Answer, and their finall patience. I had no fear but that the authors of *Smectymnuus*, to all the shew of solidity which the Remonstrant could bring, *were prepar'd both with skill and purpose to returne a suffizing answer*, and were able enough to lay the dust and pudder in antiquity, which he and his, out of stratagem, are wont to raise. But when I saw his weake arguments headed with sharpe taunts, and that his designe was, if he could not refute them, yet at least with quips and snapping adagies to vapour them out, which they bent only upon the businesse were minded to let passe; by how much I saw them taking little thought for their own injuries, I must confesse I took it as my part the lesse to endure that my respected Friends, through their own unnecessary patience, should thus lie at the mercy of a coy, flirting stile; to be girded with frumps and curtall gibes, by one who makes sentences by the Statute, as if all above three inches long were confiscate. To me it seem'd an indignity, that whom his whole wisdome could not move from their place, them his impetuous folly should presume to ride over."—*An Apology, &c.*, 1641, p. 4.

In regard to the authorship of "The Modest Confutation," Milton says, "But marke, Readers, there is a kind of justice observ'd among them that do evill, but this man loves injustice in the very order of his malice. For having all this while abus'd

<hr/>

[1] Translation in Milton's Prose Works, Bohn's edition, vol. i. p. 257.

the good name of his Adversary [Smectymnuus] with all manner
of licence in revenge of his Remonstrant, *if they be not both one
person, or,* as I am told, *Father and Son,* yet after all this he calls
for satisfaction, when as he himselfe hath already taken the utmost
farding. *Violence hath been done* (sayes he) *to the person of
a holy, and religious Prelat.* To which, something in effect to
what S. Paul answer'd of Ananias, I answer, *I wist not, Brethren,
that he was a holy and religious Prelat;* for evill is written of
those who would be Prelats. And finding him thus in disguise
without his superscription or phylactery, either of *holy* or *Prelat,*
it were no sinne to serve him as Longchamp Bishop of Elie was
serv'd in his disguise at Dover. He hath begun the measure
namelesse, and when he pleases we may all appear as we are."—
Ib. p. 20.

To this Apology for Smectymnuus, no Answer by Bishop Hall
or others appeared, and it may be said to have closed this controversy, so far as Young and the English Poet were concerned.
As for the Bishops, a Bill was passed in Parliament for the utter
Abolishing the Hierarchical form of Church government, in Sep-
tember 1642. It must be confessed that Milton, in his scornful
contempt of the claims by the English Prelates of their Apostolical Succession, of Liturgical services, and Episcopal Church Government, could not restrain himself from coarse, vehement language,
and his asperity can only be excused by keeping in view the
atrocious calumnies respecting his personal conduct which had
been circulated by his opponents.

It is scarcely worth mentioning that the name Smectymnuus
did not escape the wits of the time. In Hudibras we find a
rather far-fetched allusion to it, along with " black caps,"—

> Which Sergeants at the Gospel wear,
> To make the Spiritual calling clear,
> The Hand-kercher about the neck,
> Canonical cravat of SMECK,
> From whom the Institution came,
> When Church and State they set a flame.

(Canto III., lines 1163-66.)

A stupid enough prose tract by Henry Peacham, has the title, "A Paradox, in Praise of a Dunce, to Smectymnuus. By H. P. London, printed for Thomas Paybody, 1642," 4to., 4 leaves. It has no relation to the controversy. There also is a copy of bombastic verses by John Cleaveland, an English royalist (Lond. 1647), whose Poems, now all but forgotten, were more popular than those of Milton. The verses, included in later editions of his Poems, are entitled,—

> *Smectymnuus; or the Club Divines.*
>
> Smectymnuus! the Goblin-makes me start!
> I' th' name of Rabbi Abraham, what art?
> Syriack? or Arabick? or Welch? what skilt?
> Ap all the Bricklayers that Babel built!
> Some Conjurer translate . . .
> . . , ...
> Under each arm there's tuckt a double gyssard,
> Five faces lurke under one single vizzard.

Smectymnuus, however, survived all such attacks, and it was re-published at London, 1653, 4to, as SMECTYMNUUS REDIVIVUS, with a preface by the eminent Puritan divine, Dr Thomas Manton, which is deserving of notice—

" This Work, which the stationer has now Revived (that it may not be forgotten, and like a jewel after once shewing, shut up in the Cabinet of private studies only), was penned by [1] several worthy Divines of great note and fame in the churches of Christ, under the borrowed and covered name of SMECTYMNUUS, which was some matter of scorn and exception to the adversaries, as the Papists objected to Calvin his printing his Institutions under the name of Alcuinus, and to Bucer his naming himself Aretius Felinus, though all this without ground and reason, the Affiction of the name to any work, being a thing indifferent; for there we must not consider so much the Author, as the matter, and not who said it, but what; and the assumption of another name not being infamous, but where it is done out of deceit, and to another's prejudice, or out of shame because of guilt, or fear to own the Truths which they should establish: I suppose the

[1] *In the margin,* Mr Steven Marshall, Mr Edm. Calamy, Dr Tho. Young, Mr Matthew Newcommen, Dr Wil. Spurstowe.

Reverend Authors were willing to lie hid under this ONOMASTICK,
partly that their work might not be received with prejudice, the
faction against which they dealt, arrogating to themselves a
monopoly of learning, and condemning all others as Ignorants and
Novices not worthy to be heard; and partly that they might not
burthen their frontispiece with a voluminous nomenclature, it not
being usual to affix so many names at length to one Treatise.

" For the Work itself speaketh its own praise, and is now once
more subjected to thy censure and judgment; This second
publication of it was occasioned by another book for Vindication
of the Ministry, by the Provincial Assembly of London, wherein
there are frequent appeals to Smectymnuus; though otherwise
I should have judged the reprinting seasonable; for the Lord
hath now returned us to such a juncture of time, wherein there
is greater freedom of debate without noise and vulgar prejudice;
and certainly if the quarrel of Episcopacy were once cleared, and
brought to an issue, we should not be so much in the dark, in
other parts of Discipline," &c. . . . . . . Thine in the Lord,

THO. MANTON.

NEWINGTON, *June* 23, 1653.

Baillie, in a long letter from London to the Presbytery of
Irvine (where he was then minister), 28th February 1641, in
describing the proceedings of the Scots Commissioners, says—
"Think not we live any of us here to be idle; Mr Hendersone
hes readie now a short treatise, much called for, of our Church
Discipline; Mr Gillespie hes the grounds of Presbyteriall Government well asserted; *Mr Blair, a pertinent answer to Hall's Remonstrance:* all these are readie for the presse." (Letters and
Journals, vol. 1, p. 303.) Blair's treatise has not been identified,
and may have been superseded by Smectymnuus.

After a long interval there appeared a republication of " Smectymnuus Redivivus, &c., Composed by five Learned and Orthodox
Divines." The Sixth edition. Edinburgh, Re-printed by John
Moncur, 1708. 4to. Pp. iv. 75. It includes Dr Manton's
address as above, dated Newington, June 23, 1653.

A less successful attempt to revive this work was made in our

33

own days, as part of a collection called "The Westminster Tracts. No. I. Smectymnuus, &c. Edinburgh, 1851." 8vo. It was to have also contained, The Grand Debate, and (I presume only the first part of) Edwards' Gangræna, with notes and introduction by the Editor, who said, that such a volume, with the Westminster Standards (the Confession, Catechisms, and Form of Church Government), would "complete the Presbyterian Library, in supplying an Antidote to Diocesan Prelacy, Independency, and Doctrinal Schism." Not more, I think, than one number ever appeared. The editor was the Rev. Thomas Buchanan, minister of Methven, Perthshire. He was a good scholar, but not very conversant with the controversial literature of that time. In 1857 he obtained the degree of D.D. from the University of Glasgow, but died suddenly 24th August 1859, in his 58th year, and 27th of his ministry.

VIII.
THE SMECTYMNVVS CONTROVERSY.
1640–1642.

(1.) An Humble Remonstrance to the High Court of Parliament. By [Joseph Hall, D.D., Bishop of Exeter] a dutifull Sonne of the Church. London, printed by M. F. for Nathaniel Butter, 1640. 4to, pp. 43.

(2.) An Anti-Remonstrance, to the late Humble Remonstrance to the High Court of Parliament. Printed Anno 1641. 4to, pp. 15.

(3.) An Answer to a Book entituled An Humble Remonstrance :
In which,

The Originall of $\left\{ \begin{matrix} \text{LITURGY} \\ \text{EPISCOPACY} \end{matrix} \right\}$ is discussed.

And Queres propounded concerning both.

The Parity of Bishops and Presbyters in Scripture Demonstrated.

The Occasion of their Imparitie in Antiquitie discovered.

The Disparitie of the Ancient and our Moderne Bishops manifested.

C

The Antiquitie of Ruling Elders in the Church vindicated.
The Prelaticall Church Bownded.

Written by S M E C T Y M N V V S [viz., **Stephen Marshall, Edmund Calamy, Thomas Young, Matthew Newcomen,** and **VVilliam Spurstow.**] Printed in the yeare 1641, 4to, pp. 94.

Other copies have this imprint—

London :
Printed for J. Rothwell, and are to be sold by T. N. at the
Bible in Pope's-Head-Alley, 1641.

(4.) A Defence of the Humble Remonstrance, against the frivolous and false exceptions of SMECTYMNVVS. Wherein the right of Liturgie and Episcopacie is clearly vindicated from the vaine cavils and challenges of the Answerers. By [Bishop Hall] the Author of the said Humble Remonstrance. Seconded (in way of appendance) with the judgement of the famous Divine of the Palatinate, D. Abrahamus Scultetus, late Professor of Divinitie in the Universitie of Heidelberg : Concerning the Divine Right of Episcopacie, and the No-right of Lay-Eldership. Faithfully translated out of his Latine. London, printed for Nathaniel Butter, 1641, 4to, pp. 200. [but only 190 pages, 183-192 being omitted].

(5.) A Vindication of the Answer to the Humble Remonstrance, from the unjust imputations of frivolousnesse and falsehood : Wherein

$$\text{The cause of} \left\{ \begin{array}{c} \text{Liturgy} \\ \text{and} \\ \text{Episcopacy} \end{array} \right\} \text{ is further debated.}$$

By the same SMECTYMNVVS. London, printed for John Rothwell, 1641, 4to, pp. [xv.] and 219.

(6.) A Short Answer to the Tedious Vindication of SMECTYMNVVS. By the Author of the Humble Remonstrance. London, printed for Nathaniel Butter, 1641, 4to, pp. [xvi.] and 103.

(7.) The Reason of Church-governement urg'd against Prelaty. By Mr John Milton. In two books. London, printed by E. G., for John Rothwell, 1641, 4to, pp. 65.

(8.) The Originall of Bishops and Metropolitans, briefly laid downe by James Ussher, sometime Professor of Divinity in the

University of Dublin, and afterwards Archbishop of Armagh, and Primate of all Ireland. Oxford, 1641, 4to.

(9.) The Iudgement of Doctor Rainoldes touching the Originall of Episcopacy. More largely confirmed out of Antiquity by James Archbishop of Armagh. London, printed by G. M. for Thomas Dovvnes. 1641, 4to, title, and pp. 16.

(10.) Of Prelatical Episcopacy, and Whither it may be deduc'd from the Apostolical times, by vertue of those Testimonies which are alledg'd to that purpose in some late Treatises ; one whereof goes under the name of Iames Arch-bishop of Armagh. [By John Milton.] London, printed by R. O. & G. D. for Thomas Under-hill, 1641, 4to, pp. 24.

(11.) Animadversions upon the Remonstrant's Defence against SMECTYMNVVS. [By John Milton.] London, printed for Thomas Underhill, 1641, 4to, pp. 68.

(12.) A Modest Confutation of a Slanderous and Scurrilous Libell, entituled, Animadversions upon the Remonstrants Defense against Smectymnuus, Printed in the yeer M.DC.XLII., 4to. title, 4 pages To the Reader, and pp. 40.

(13.) An Apology against a pamphlet call'd, A Modest Con-futation of the Animadversions upon the Remonstrant against SMECTYMNUUS. [By John Milton]. London, printed by E. G., for John Rothwell, 1642, 4to, pp. 59.

The unsold copies of this tract were, twelve years later, re-issued with a new title, An Apology for SMECTYMNVVS, with the Reason of Church Government. By John Meltom (*sic*), Gent. London, printed for John Rothwell, 1654, 4to. pp. 65.

IX.

THE WESTMINSTER ASSEMBLY OF DIVINES, 1643.

This celebrated Assembly, by virtue of an ordinance of the Lords and Commons, notwithstanding the King's prohibition, met on the 1st of June 1643, and included ten Lords and twenty Commoners, as Lay Assessors. The Minutes, partly in rough scrolls by the Scribe of the Assembly, are preserved in Dr Williams's library, London, and have been copied with the view of publication, in whole or in part, by a Committee of the General

Assembly of the Church of Scotland. I have been kindly favoured by the Rev. John Struthers, minister of Prestonpans, one of the acting Committee, with the following extracts relating to Dr Thomas Young. The Journal or Notes of the Assembly's proceedings, by Dr Lightfoot and George Gillespie, are now easily accessible in a printed form.

Two other books on the subject may be noticed. The History of the Westminster Assembly of Divines, by the Rev. W. M. Hetherington, 1843; and Memoirs of the Divines, &c., by the Rev. James Reid, Paisley, 1811, 1815. 2 vols. 8vo.

Excerpts from Notes of Westminster Assembly Debates (Vol. First, from August 4, 1643, to April 11, 1644), wherein Thomas Young, one of the Commissioners to that Assembly, appears, especially on questions of Ecclesiastical Antiquity, to have taken an active part—

I. In the debate *on the Lay element in the ancient Jewish Sanhedrim*, which took place on December 13, 1643 (as noted in MS. f. 2666, or in transcript p. 524), says, "Mr Young.—The place is Deut. xvii. 8, and the question whether it holds out two courts, or but one. . . . It is granted that [there was] but one court, and in that court a mixture of several persons, and the causes merely civil" [?] [I infer] "from that place two courts." [Because]

1. Two several causes of several sorts or natures, 'blood and blood, and plea and plea.' Those both of civil causes . . . between stroke and stroke, or plague and plague, that is, in causes of another nature, unclean.

2. According to the distinction of causes, a distinction of judges . . .

In the 12th verse, [the judicial authorities are] apparently distinguished. [We have in] "*or*" under the judge a disjunctive article . . . Appeals well spoken to . . . if any case or doubt concerning spiritual matters, to whom shall they go to be determined [?] shall they go to the civil [tribunal]? No! The priest's lips to preserve knowledge." [Mal. ii. 7.]

II. In debate on the *Office of Deacon*, as grounded on Acts vi.

1–4, under date December 15, 1643, notes in Tr. p. 544, says, "Mr Young—The question was whether office of deacons held out in the history of Acts vi. . . . and whether perpetual . . . Concerning the first, a learned account given by my brother . . I shall not need to repeat . . . either acceptation of the word . . . only insist a little upon the very phrase διακονεῖν τραπέζεις. Some learned men, considering the use of that phrase, have enquired after the sense of it . . . and considered of two uses . . . The Deacons [they say were] appointed—

1. To consider to see that there might be a decorum kept in the congregations of Christians.

2. To take care of the poor.

For the first, Beza's judgment is . . . in that age of Apostles, in all their meetings they did not only administer the sacrament of the Lord's Supper, but did also feast together, as appears [from] 1 Cor. xi., where, besides the sacrament of the Lord's Supper, there is mention of their proper supper. He was to observe the proper decorum in both these things.

[For the] second, Holy conference. Another duty. A receiving of the benevolence of Christians of what nature soever it was, whether ample or otherwise, as God blessed them.

Here, then, being three things that fall out, the Deacon had a principal charge to see to two of these. Thereupon it is that Baronius grants what I affirm, and censures [confirms?] it by a testimony out of Chrysostom . . . in the age next to the Apostles it continued. Justin Martyr, the deacon [was] employed for transporting of the consecrated elements to them that were sick, and Tertullian the late passage [probably meaning that Tertullian was the authority for the last passage]. Whosoever of the ancients commonly speak of this office [of deacon] they have a reference to this place [Acts vi. 1–4].

For the ministry of the word at first institution, three good reasons given, especially the second, it was not fit for them to leave the word and serve tables . . . If not fit for the Apostles, much more unfit for another . . . True, Stephen preached, but in such an assembly that any [one] might . . . True, Philip did administer the sacrament [of baptism], but [he was] then termed Philip the Evangelist . . .

Afterwards the Church admitted into some degrees, but first they were the men that did use to read the Scripture . . So in Ciprian's time Optatus . . . Therefore, I do think that first they were called to attend upon the necessities of the church . . . for that of order, in succeeding times the deacon gave the word for ordering of all things . . . Athanasius, when the church [was] compassed about with soldiers to apprehend him, gave order to the deacon to call out for a prayer, saith one, —a psalm, saith another.

So then here is an office [instituted for it] by Apostles.

2. This word Diaconus is used by Apostle contradistinct to all them that labour in word and doctrine.

3. Consider the use of it in the primitive Church . . . from lectors and inferior places they did ascend to higher, and so they came first to assist in the sacrament, but they were not to consecrate, yet afterwards they came to be the same . . . Ministering to the saints, it is every [where] used in the Scriptures for the supplying the necessities of the poor. 1 Cor. xvi. [15] the house of Stephanus . . . Lay all these together . . . for the perpetuity of it . . .

[N.B.—This speech of Young's is not noticed at all in Light-foot's Notes.—J. S.]

III. In the debate as to the *Pastor visiting the Sick*, under date December 19, 1643 (as noted in transcript, p. 552), says, " Mr Young—Concerning this proposition, whether he be bound *ex officio* to do it, whether solely his duty ; the proposition does not determine.

Concerning custom of foreign churches . . . Concerning Lutherans, every one that is the Confessor of the party, he is tied to come to him what disease soever sick of.

I do remember in Zancheus upon the Phil. [he] hath this very question now before us . . . Zanchy concluded against them . . . This proposition as now it lies in Divinity cannot be denied. One branch of God's complaint against the false people [prophets?] is that . . . [they had scattered his flock, and had not visited them. Jer. xxiii. 2].

IV. In the debate on *Church Government*, under date 21st February 1643-4, as very briefly noted (at pp. 621-29, transcript), Mr Young replied to Mr Selden and others, by citations from the Fathers, in support of the Presbyterian system, which they sought to combat by arguments thence derived.

V. In the debate on the *Multitude of Teachers and Congregations in the Church at Jerusalem*, under date 26th February 1643-4, (as noted in transcript, p. 660), says, " Mr Young—It might be remembered that it had been suggested that the meetings in the temple were not properly meetings of Christians . . . being converted, where did they meet afterwards? The text [Acts ii. 46] saith from house to house, [*i.e.* there were] private meetings in respect of the public [ones] which the Jews then had [in their synagogues or in the temple].

1643-4, March 15.—A letter read from Earl of Manchester, stating that he cast out Drs Beale, Cosins, Sterne, Martin, Laney, Masters from their Masterships in Cambridge University, and subject to the Assembly's approval nominated Mr Palmer, Mr Arrowsmith, Mr Vines, Mr Seaman, and *Mr Young* in their places. The Assembly offered their congratulations, but desired that their brethren should meanwhile not be withdrawn from the Assembly. [Dr Lightfoot, p. 218, says, " Mr Vines and Mr Young wished to be excused, but though a long account is given in the notes of a speech by Mr Ash, who delivered Lord Manchester's letter as to what had been done, towards administering the Covenant in the several colleges, &c." In the MS. no mention is made of the declinature of Mr Vines or Mr Young.—J. S.]

PRINTED BY NEILL AND COMPANY, EDINBURGH.